Fashion Fun

ROSIE BAN

Wishing Star Palace

The Secret Princess Promise

"I promise that I will be kind and brave,

Using my magic to help and save,

Granting wishes and doing my best,

To make people smile and bring happiness."

CONTENTS

CHAPTER ONE

Playtime at the Palace

"Can anyone tell me the capital of France?"
Miss Kelly asked.

Mia Thompson and her classmates were
sitting at their desks having a French
lesson. A map of France was projected on
the whiteboard and the teacher was holding
a stripy blue, white and red flag.

Before Mia could put her hand up to

 11

answer, a boy with a crop of messy brown
hair put up his own hand and shouted out,
"Paris!"

"*Oui!* That's correct, Thomas," said Miss
Kelly. "But next time please remember to
wait to be called before answering," she
reminded him gently.

They had only been back at school for
a few days, but Mia's new teacher seemed
really kind.

Mia's favourite subject at school was art, but she also really liked French lessons – learning how to speak a new language was exciting! So far, Miss Kelly had taught the

class how to count to ten and they'd learned a song about the days of the week.

A girl named Emily who was sitting next to Mia waved her hand in the air. When the teacher called on her, she said, "I went to Paris on my summer holiday."

"Would you like to tell us about it?" Miss Kelly asked.

"It was really beautiful," said Emily. "We went to the top of the Eiffel Tower and my mum and dad ate snails!"

"Ewwww!" cried the other children.

Miss Kelly smiled. "France is famous for many things – art, perfume, fashion and delicious food. It sounds like you had a wonderful holiday, Emily."

Mia grinned as she started daydreaming about her own summer holiday. She and her family had visited her best friend, Charlotte. Charlotte used to live in the UK and go to the same school as Mia, until her family moved to California. It had been amazing to spend time with Charlotte and to see where she lived now.

They'd gone to the beach, visited a theme park and eaten hot dogs at a baseball game. When it had been time for them to go, everyone had expected Mia and Charlotte to be sad about saying goodbye.

But Mia knew she'd see Charlotte again soon – somewhere even more exciting than California ... a magical place called Wishing Star Palace!

Just before Charlotte had moved to America, the girls' old babysitter, Alice, had given them magic necklaces shaped like half-hearts. Alice had explained that both girls had the potential to become Secret Princesses – who made wishes come true using magic!

With every wish they granted, the girls were getting closer to becoming fully fledged Secret Princesses. Not long ago, Mia and Charlotte had passed their second stage of training and earned a truly brilliant reward – sparkling ruby slippers that let them travel magically to any place they wanted to go! *I wonder where our ruby slippers will take us next*, thought Mia, twirling her blonde hair around her finger. She imagined all the different places she and Charlotte could visit – a rainforest, a sandy desert, the Arctic Circle …

BRRRRIIIINNNG! A bell startled Mia out of her daydream.

"Break time!" announced Miss Kelly.

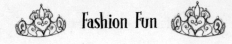

Mia's classmates rushed out of the classroom and charged into the playground.

"Let's play cops and robbers!" shouted Thomas. "I'm a robber!"

"Want to be on our team, Mia?" asked Emily, waving her over. Mia smiled and ran over to join Emily's team.

When Charlotte had been in their class, she was always picked first for games. Charlotte was a fast runner and good at sports. Thinking about her best friend, Mia pulled her gold pendant out from under her collar. To her amazement, it was glowing!

"Er, I forgot something," Mia told Emily. "I'll be right back." She ran back inside her empty classroom.

When she was sure
she was alone,
Mia held her half-
heart pendant
and said, "I
wish I could see
Charlotte!" The
pendant glowed
even brighter,
filling Mia's
cheerful classroom
with dazzling
light. The light
swirled around
Mia and then
– *WHOOSH!*

Fashion Fun

The magic whisked her away from school.
Mia wasn't worried about missing her next
lesson. She knew that no time would pass
while she was having a magical adventure.

Mia landed in an entrance hall with
marble pillars and a sweeping staircase. Her
school uniform had magically transformed
into an outfit just right for a palace – a
golden princess dress, a diamond tiara and
sparkling ruby slippers!

"Looking good, Mia!" a familiar voice
called out.

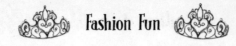

Mia turned around and saw a girl with curly brown hair in a pale pink princess dress. The only thing that shone brighter than her diamond tiara and her ruby slippers was the smile on her face.

"You too, Charlotte!" said Mia, running over to hug her best friend.

"I was at school when my pendant started glowing," said Mia. "We had just gone outside for morning break."

"Cool!" said Charlotte, grinning. "Recess is the best thing about school." Since moving to California, she had started using some American expressions. Playtime was called recess there!

"I wonder if the princesses have gone

outside, too?" Mia joked. She peeked into a
few rooms leading off the entrance hall, but
there were no princesses in the throne room,
the dining room or the ballroom.

"I was hoping we could start the next
stage of our training today," said Charlotte.

"Me too," said Mia, her blue eyes
sparkling. "I want to earn my sapphire
ring!"

Like their ruby slippers, the princesses'
sapphire rings had magical powers! The
blue jewels flashed when danger was nearby,
and they glowed in the dark. But the girls
needed to grant four people's wishes in order
to complete the next stage of their training
and get princess rings of their very own.

"I know," said Charlotte, wriggling her fingers in anticipation. "Rings that warn us of danger would be really handy when we're having an adventure!"

Mia's forehead suddenly wrinkled in concern. "You don't suppose the princesses are in danger now, do you?"

To her relief, she heard a familiar voice calling them. "Mia! Charlotte! Come and join us upstairs!"

"Come on," said Charlotte, her hazel eyes flashing with excitement. "Let's go and find out why they called us here!"

CHAPTER TWO

The Princesses' Portraits

"Coming!" called Charlotte. She and Mia
bounded up the staircase.

They found the Secret Princesses gathered
on the landing at the top of the stairs.

"Welcome back, girls," said a princess.
Her strawberry-blonde hair had cool red
streaks in it. She hugged them both. "How
was your summer?"

 25

"Hi, Alice," said Mia, hugging her back. "It was amazing."

"We had sooooo much fun together," Charlotte told her.

"We're so happy to be back at Wishing Star Palace, though," said Mia, her eyes shining with excitement. "We can't wait to start the next stage of our training."

"You will soon, I promise," said Princess Alice, tugging a lock of Mia's hair playfully. "We brought you here today because Princess Sophie needs your help."

"Do you need us to grant a wish?" Charlotte asked Sophie eagerly.

"No," said Sophie. She was wearing a paint-splattered apron over her princess dress. "I need help making a decision."

"Sophie's been chosen to show her paintings at a brand new art gallery called the Hexagon," Alice told them proudly, putting her arm around Sophie's shoulder.

"Well done!" said Charlotte.

"That's great," said Mia. The exhibition sounded like a really big deal for Sophie.

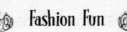
"Thanks," said Sophie modestly. "I've chosen some paintings from my studio at home, but I want to include some of the portraits I've painted of the princesses." She fiddled with her necklace. It had a paintbrush pendant, showing that her special talent was art. "But I just can't decide which ones to choose. Will you help me pick?"

"Of course!" said Charlotte.

The other princesses headed downstairs while the girls followed Sophie to the portrait gallery. It was a long corridor lined with paintings of every Secret Princesses that had ever been. Some of them were in antique frames and showed princesses

from long ago. But like the modern-day
Secret Princesses, all of the princesses in the
paintings wore necklaces that showed their
special talent.

"Look, there's Florence and Esme," said
Mia, pointing to a portrait
of two girls in old-
fashioned dresses.
They were
Friendship
Princesses
and had
half-heart
pendants
just like
Mia

and Charlotte. They were the most powerful type of Secret Princess because they always worked together, but they were also the rarest. There hadn't been any Friendship Princesses since Florence and Esme ... until now!

Moving down the corridor, they came to the more recent portraits. Several of them had been painted by Sophie.

"I love this one," said Mia, admiring a portrait of Princess Ella with a fluffy white kitten on her lap. Ella was a vet and you could see how much she loved animals from the way she was gently stroking the kitten.

"You were painting that the first time we visited the palace," said Charlotte.

30

"That's right," said Sophie, smiling.

"Alice looks so glamorous in her portrait," said Mia. The picture showed the pop star princess singing into a microphone, light glinting off her pendant shaped like a musical note.

They came to an empty frame. Mia shuddered. The frame had once held a portrait of Princess Poison, painted when she was still a Secret Princess. Princess Poison had been banished from Wishing Star Palace for using wishes for herself instead of helping others. Now, she did everything she could to spoil wishes, so that she could become more powerful. It was very hard to believe that the cruel, spiteful woman who tried to stop Mia and Charlotte from granting wishes had ever been worthy of her wand. Secret Princesses were brave, kind and loyal – everything that Princess Poison wasn't!

"But why is the frame still here?" Charlotte asked.

Sophie thought for a moment. "It reminds us that being a Secret Princess is a wonderful privilege," she said. "And of everything we'd lose if we didn't honour our Secret Princess promise."

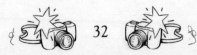

If I become a Secret Princess, Mia thought, *I'll never forget how lucky I am.* She imagined a picture of herself and Charlotte hanging in the gallery, just like Florence and Esme – it would be so amazing!

"I need to pick four portraits to go to the gallery," Sophie said.

"How are you going to choose?" Charlotte asked Sophie. "They're all so beautiful."

Princess Sophie sighed. "I don't know!" she said. "All the princesses are my friends. I love them all dearly and I don't want to choose between them."

"You don't want to hurt anyone's feelings," said Mia sympathetically.

Sophie nodded.

"Then why don't you leave it to chance?" suggested Charlotte.

"What do you mean?" asked Sophie.

"Turn on the light in your sapphire ring," said Charlotte, "and shut your eyes. Mia and I will spin you around and when you come to a stop, pick the portrait the light is pointing to."

"That's a brilliant idea!" Sophie exclaimed. She tapped the sparkling blue stone on her ring and a soft glow shone out of it. Sophie shut her eyes and the girls spun her around – one … two … three times.

The light from Sophie's ring was pointing at a portrait of a princess with bright red

hair holding an amazing cake in the shape
of Wishing Star Palace.

"Princess Sylvie!" said Mia.

The girls spun Sophie round again. This
time, the light from her ring shone on a
portrait of a princess in a purple leotard.

Her arms were stretched over her head as if she was just about to launch into a gymnastics routine.

"And Princess Kiko!" said Charlotte.

Sophie shut her eyes and the girls spun her around once more. The ring's beam of blue light fell on a portrait of a princess wearing a funky tropical

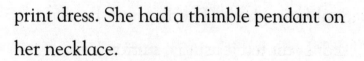

print dress. She had a thimble pendant on her necklace.

"Princess Cara's portrait is a great choice," said Mia.

"One more to go," said Charlotte.

"I'm feeling a bit dizzy," Sophie said, clutching her tummy. "I don't think I can take any more spinning."

There was still one more painting to choose. Mia looked down the line and caught sight of a portrait of Sophie herself, holding a paint palette. The artist had perfectly captured her delicate freckles and the copper highlights in her hair.

"Who painted your portrait?" Mia asked Sophie. "It's lovely."

Sophie laughed. "Thank you," she said. "I did. I painted it using a mirror."

"Why don't you bring that one?" suggested Charlotte.

"Are you sure?" asked Sophie.

"Definitely," Mia and Charlotte said together.

Charlotte leaned over the banister and shouted down the stairs. "Everyone! We've made a decision!"

The princesses hurried back upstairs.

"Sylvie, Kiko and Cara, could I please include your portraits in my show?" asked Princess Sophie.

"Of course!" said Princess Cara.

"It would be an honour!" Sylvie said.

Princess Kiko nodded happily.

"But weren't you supposed to pick four?" asked Alice.

"She's taking her self-portrait, too," explained Mia.

"That's a brilliant idea," exclaimed Alice.

Smiling, Sophie waved her wand. There was a flash of sparkling light and suddenly she, Cara, Sylvie and Kiko were all holding their portraits!

"Whoa! What's going on?" Kiko asked.

"I thought you three might like to come with me to the gallery," said Sophie. "So you can see your portraits on display."

Sylvie, Cara and Kiko all exchanged excited looks.

"We'd love to come!" cried Sylvie as the others nodded.

"Have fun," said Charlotte.

"Please let us know how the show goes," said Mia.

"We won't need to," said Sophie, with a grin. "Because you two are coming with us!"

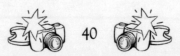

CHAPTER THREE
The Hexagon

Mia and Charlotte stared at Sophie. They couldn't believe their ears.

"For real?" asked Mia.

Sophie nodded. "But only if you want to come."

"Are you kidding?" asked Charlotte. "Yes, please!"

Mia looked down at her ruby slippers.

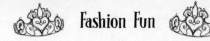
"Where are we going, exactly?" she asked Princess Sophie, getting ready to click her heels together.

"To the Hexagon art gallery," Sophie replied. "But we aren't going to use our shoes to get there." She beckoned the others to follow her downstairs. Sophie opened the palace doors and led them out into the gardens.

"Oh my gosh!" exclaimed Mia.

A hot-air balloon was waiting for them on the lush, green lawn! It had pink and lilac stripes and there was a big wicker basket suspended beneath it.

"Come on! Let's get in," Princess Sophie suggested.

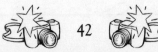

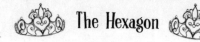

The girls didn't need telling
twice. Lifting up her long
skirt, Charlotte climbed
nimbly into the basket.
Mia scrambled in right
behind her.

"We'll help you
get in," Charlotte
told the other
princesses.

One by one, they helped Sophie, Cara, Sylvie and Kiko into the basket, carefully holding the portraits while the princesses climbed in.

"It's tricky in a gown," said Princess Sylvie, laughing as she swung her legs over the edge of the basket.

Once all the princesses and paintings were safely in the basket, Sophie took out her wand and waved it. Pink sparkles flew out of the tip and swirled around the balloon.

Then it rose up into the air!

"Yay!" cheered Mia and Charlotte, peering over the side of the basket as the hot-air balloon gently floated above the palace grounds.

Alice and the other princesses had gathered on the lawn to see them off. "Goodbye!" they called, blowing kisses to their departing friends.

As the balloon climbed higher and higher in the sky, Mia and Charlotte waved until

 45

the princesses down on the ground looked
like tiny dots.

"This is so cool," said Charlotte, as they
floated through the clouds.

"Well, prepare to get hot," said Sophie,
winking. She waved her wand again and
pink sparkles danced around the basket.
A jet of flames appeared underneath the
balloon and the temperature in the basket
rose. Mia felt her cheeks flushing.

"We left Wishing Star Palace by magic,"
explained Sophie. "But now that we're back
in the real world, we need hot air to power
the balloon."

"But our clothes are the same!" cried
Mia, looking down at her outfit. Everyone's

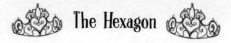

tiaras had vanished, but they still had their beautiful princess dresses on.

"It's a special occasion at the gallery," Sophie said. "So it'll be nice to be dressed up!"

"Yay, I love being dressed up!" said Cara.

"You always look lovely," said Sophie, grinning. Cara was a fashion designer who wore very cool clothing.

"Hey! Is that the Hexagon?" called Kiko, looking over the side of the basket.

Below them, a glass building was gleaming in the sunlight.

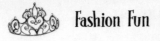

"I think you're right," said Sophie. She pulled a cord that opened the top of the balloon, letting some of the hot air out. The balloon started to sink down towards the ground.

"Now I see why it's called the Hexagon," said Mia. She remembered from maths lessons at school that hexagons had six sides. From the air, they could see all six sides of the building.

The balloon landed outside the gallery with a gentle bump. The princesses climbed out of the basket with the girls' help, taking care to keep Princess Sophie's precious portraits safe.

The Hexagon's green-tinted glass walls

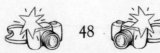

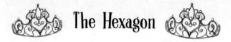
rose up before them. Outside there was a
sign that said *New Show! Exclusive look at
paintings by Sophie Peters.*

"Look, there's your name!" said Kiko,
nudging Sophie.

Wide doors slid open automatically and
they all walked into the gallery excitedly.

"Are you Sophie?" asked a teenage girl holding a walkie-talkie. She tucked her short black hair nervously behind her ear.

"Yes, that's me," said Sophie, shaking the girl's hand. "My friends and I are just delivering a few paintings for the exhibition."

"Let me take those for you," the girl said, hurrying to collect the four portraits.

"What a wonderful space," said Sophie, gazing around. Sunlight was streaming through the glass. "Have the paintings from my studio arrived yet?" she asked the girl.

"Er, yes. Um, I think so," said the girl, sounding flustered.

"Poor thing," Mia whispered to Charlotte.

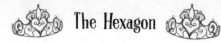

"She's probably nervous because this is the gallery's first show."

The girl murmured something into her walkie-talkie and a short man in a boiler suit and a hard hat came into the gallery holding a ladder. He quickly began to hang up the four portraits up on the walls.

Sophie directed the man anxiously as he struggled to hold up the paintings. He didn't seem very good at it at all! As Sophie pointed, Mia saw a beam of blue light hit the glass wall.

"What's that?" she asked Charlotte. The light seemed to be flashing.

"It's Sophie's ring!" Charlotte said. "There must be danger nearby!"

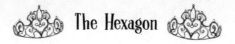

Before they could warn Sophie, a tall, thin woman in a tight green suit walked into the gallery. She had long, black hair with an ice-blonde streak and cold green eyes.

"Princess Poison!" gasped Mia.

"Welcome to my gallery," said Princess Poison, smirking. "I named it after someone very dear to me."

The man in the boiler suit had finished hanging the last portrait. He climbed down from his ladder and whipped off his hard hat. It was Hex, Princess Poison's nasty servant! The girls gasped as they realised the Hexagon was named after him!

"You've met Jinx already," said Princess Poison, pointing her wand at the girl.

"She's my new trainee!" Princess Poison crossed the gallery, her high heels clicking, and put her arm around Jinx. "I figured since the Silly Princesses have annoying trainees, I should have one too! I'm teaching her how to spoil wishes. Soon she will be very powerful –
just like me."

Jinx smiled
nervously.

"Why do
you want
the pictures
of Secret
Princesses?"
Charlotte asked.

"You don't even like them."

"Excellent question," said Princess Poison in a smug voice. "Naturally I didn't want the portraits so that I could look at them. No, it was so I could curse them."

The four princesses stared at Princess Poison blankly. *Why aren't they doing something?* Mia thought desperately.

"As long as their paintings all hang in my gallery, Sophie, Sylvie, Kiko and Cara won't remember that they are Secret Princesses," said Princess Poison with a snigger.

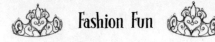
Hex chuckled gleefully.

"What's more, they won't even believe in magic any more!" Princess Poison said triumphantly.

Mia gasped.

"No!" shouted Charlotte, sprinting over to the portrait of Princess Sylvie. She desperately tried to pull it off the wall, but it was stuck fast.

"Try all you like," Princess Poison sneered. "There's only one way for the curse to be broken. If the princesses return to Wishing Star Palace, so will their portraits." She laughed cruelly. "But that will never happen because they don't even remember that it exists!"

 56

"Do something, Sophie!" Mia cried. "You can't let her keep your paintings!"

"What do you mean?" Sophie asked her, looking puzzled. "It's an honour to have my own show at the Hexagon."

Charlotte tugged Sylvie's hand urgently.

"Sylvie, we need to go back to Wishing
Star Palace!"

Sylvie laughed and squeezed Charlotte's
hand. "Sorry, little girl, I don't have time to
play right now."

Mia and Charlotte looked at each other
in dismay. They turned to Cara and Kiko.

"You are Secret Princesses," Mia said,
willing them to understand.

"You need to use your magic to get out of
here NOW!" added Charlotte.

"You two are so cute," said Kiko, smiling
at the girls. "I used to love pretending to be
a princess when I was little."

"I'd love to be a princess, but I'm a
fashion designer," Cara told the girls kindly.

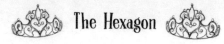
"I wish we could do magic – it would make our jobs a lot easier!"

All of the princesses laughed.

"This is terrible," Mia said to Charlotte. "They think we're making it all up."

"That's right," said Princess Poison smugly. "My curse is already working beautifully." She strode around the gallery, inspecting the four portraits.

"Let's go back to Wishing Star Palace," Charlotte whispered to Mia. "The other princesses will know what to do."

The girls held hands and clicked the heels of their sparkling slippers. "Wishing Star Palace!" they called out.

"Stop them!" shouted Princess Poison.

Hex and Jinx sprinted towards the girls but it was too late. The magic was already whisking Mia and Charlotte away.

"Don't worry!" Mia called out as they left the princesses behind. "We're going to get help!"

CHAPTER FOUR
Lena's Wish

The girls landed in the grounds of Wishing Star Palace. A group of princesses were sitting in the sunshine, having tea together.

"Hi, girls," said Alice happily. "Where are all the others?"

"Princess Poison!" Charlotte blurted out. "She's put a horrible curse on the portraits! Sophie, Sylvie, Cara and Kiko don't

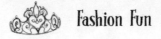
remember that they are Secret Princesses."

"They don't even believe in magic any more!" Mia felt tears welling up in her eyes. Princess Poison had done lots of bad things, but this was the worst!

"Hang on a minute," said Princess Ella, frowning in dismay. "What was Princess Poison doing there?"

"The Hexagon is her gallery!" cried Charlotte. "The whole thing was just a trick to curse the portraits."

"As long as the paintings are hanging in the Hexagon, the princesses won't remember anything about Wishing Star Palace," explained Mia. "We have to bring them back here to break the spell."

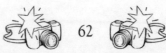

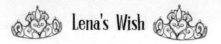

Ella put down the teapot she was holding. "That's terrible," she said, her face pale.

"We have to help them," said Princess Evie, pushing her plate of cake away.

"We tried!" cried Mia. "We begged them to come back here with us but they thought we were making it all up."

"What can we do?"
Charlotte asked the princesses
desperately.

Princess Anna, the oldest
and wisest of the Secret
Princesses, thought for a
moment. "There's only
one thing we CAN do,"
she said.

"What?" Mia asked her.

"Make them believe in
magic again," replied
Anna. "If we show
them that magic is
real, we can convince
them to come back to

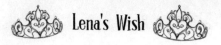

Wishing Star Palace and break the spell."

"I don't think it will be easy," said Mia, biting her lip. "They don't remember anything about this place."

Alice smiled at Mia kindly. "If anyone can help them, it's our two amazing trainee princesses."

Just then, all the princesses' wands started to glow.

"Someone has a wish that needs granting," said Charlotte.

"Can we go?" begged Mia. "We really want to help after what happened at the Hexagon."

Charlotte nodded. "Granting wishes is the least we can do."

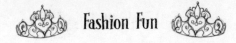

"Of course," said Alice. "It's a chance to start the next stage of your training, too."

Right now, earning her sapphire ring was the furthest thing from Mia's mind. She just wanted to help the princesses!

Mia and Charlotte ran into the palace.

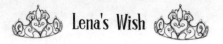
They raced up the spiral staircase to the
Mirror Room. At the top of the turret there
was a small room, empty except for an oval
mirror. Mia and Charlotte touched the
cloudy glass and a rhyme appeared.
Mia read it out:

"Your next stage of
training has begun,
Four bright blue
jewels must
now be won.
Grant four wishes
and happiness bring,
Then you will earn a
sapphire ring!"

Mia and Charlotte touched the mirror
again and an image of a
teenage girl appeared.
She had long,
dark-blonde hair
and was wearing
a trendy outfit
– a sparkly top,
ripped jeans and
cool gold ankle
boots. She was
picking at one of
the rips on her jeans
nervously. She looked very pretty – but also
very lonely.

"Let's find out who she is," said Charlotte.

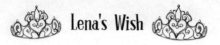

The girls touched the mirror again and more words magically appeared.

"A wish needs granting, adventures await,
Call Lena's name, don't hesitate!"

Mia and Charlotte both said, "Lena," at the same time. The glass swirled with light. They touched the mirror, and Mia felt the magic pulling them into a tunnel of light.

They landed in a beautiful garden with formal flowerbeds and a fountain with toy sailboats floating in it. There were lots of people strolling along the paths, but thanks to the magic, nobody noticed them arrive out of thin air.

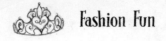

Mia looked down and saw that she was wearing a pretty floral dress and a little cardigan. Charlotte had on a striped top, cropped trousers and a red scarf tied jauntily around her neck.

"Cute outfits!" said Charlotte, flicking her scarf over her shoulder.

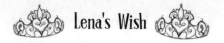

The girls stepped aside to let a family pushing a baby buggy go past them. The mother smiled and murmured, "*Merci.*"

"They're not speaking English," Charlotte said to Mia, looking puzzled. "I wonder where we are."

Mia looked around. She spotted a tower

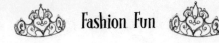

in the distance. "Charlotte!" she said excitedly. "We're in Paris, in France!" She pointed at the tower. "That's the Eiffel Tower – I just learned about it at school."

"Awesome!" said Charlotte. Then she frowned. "What if Lena doesn't speak English? How will we able to help her?"

"Let's worry about that once we've found her," said Mia.

They scanned the park. Over by the flowerbeds, a photographer was taking pictures of a cool-looking girl with dyed blue hair in two buns. She was wearing a tutu and high-heeled sandals that laced around her ankles. Someone was brushing powder on her face.

"Wow, my mum would never let me have shoes like that!" Charlotte said.

"Neither would mine!" Mia said with a grin. "It looks like a fashion photo shoot. But that's not the girl from the mirror."

"No, but that's her," said Charlotte, nodding towards a bench where Lena was sitting, looking sad.

Charlotte and Mia walked over to Lena.

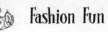

"Um, *bonjour*," said Mia nervously, trying out the French word for hello.

"*Bonjour*," Lena replied. Then she smiled and said, "I'm sorry, but that's about all the French I know."

"Same here!" said Mia, relieved that Lena spoke English. "I'm learning it at school back in England."

"That's where I'm from too," said Lena. "Actually, I was born in Poland but I moved to England with my mum when I was little."

"So what are you doing in Paris?" asked Charlotte, curiously.

"I'm in a contest," explained Lena. "I made it to the finals of the *Teen Style* magazine fashion competition for best

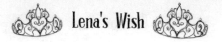

young stylist." She smiled shyly.

"Congratulations!" said Mia.

"Did you make your outfit?" asked Charlotte. "It's really cool."

Lena nodded. "My mum taught me how to sew when I was little. I really want to be a famous fashion designer one day."

"If your outfit is anything to go by, you should have a really good chance of winning," said Charlotte.

"Thanks," said Lena. "But the other two finalists are really good, too. We're all getting our pictures taken for the magazine."

Mia looked over at the photographer, who was now taking pictures of a girl with a

blonde bob wearing a sleek silver jumpsuit.

"I really hope I win," Lena told them. "The prize is a place at the Central Fashion Academy in Paris. It's the best fashion school in the world! It's all I've ever wished for."

Mia and Charlotte exchanged looks. They knew what Lena's wish was – to win the contest. Now they could get on with helping her!

"It's your turn, Lena," said one of the photographer's assistants. "Jean-Pierre wants to photograph you by the fountain."

"Is it OK if we watch?" asked Charlotte.

"Sure," said Lena. "My mum had to stay at home to look after my little sisters.

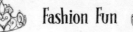

It would be great to have some company."

Lena posed on the edge of the fountain. An assistant came over and put some lipstick and blusher on her face, while another brushed her hair.

"OK," exclaimed Jean-Pierre the photographer, who had a heavy French accent. "Give me a big smile, Lena."

As Lena smiled for the camera, a dark-haired girl suddenly came running over to the fountain. She bumped into Lena.

"Whoa!" yelled Lena, struggling to keep her balance. She teetered on the edge of the fountain, then fell backwards into the water with a big SPLASH!

CHAPTER FIVE
Say Cheese

"Lena!" cried Mia. She and Charlotte ran over to the fountain and pulled Lena out of the water. Her hair was dripping wet and her clothes were completely soaked.

"Oh no!" Lena wailed, pushing wet hair out of her face. "My outfit is ruined!"

Mia spun around and saw the girl who had bumped into Lena staring at them.

 79

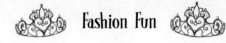
It was Jinx, Princess Poison's new trainee!

"Why did you do that?" Mia demanded.

"That wasn't very nice at all."

Jinx opened her mouth as if she was going
to say something, but she changed her
mind. She turned and ran away through

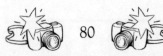

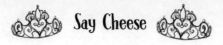

the garden. The girls didn't bother to chase after her – Lena needed their help!

Jean-Pierre came over and handed Lena a towel. "Do you have a change of clothes?" he asked her.

Lena shook her head. "Sorry," she replied. "I didn't think I'd need one."

The photographer took off his hat and rubbed his head. "Well, I can't photograph you looking like that," he said.

"Maybe we could run to a clothes store and buy Lena a new outfit," suggested Charlotte.

Jean-Pierre shook his head. "I'm afraid that is not possible," he said. "The three finalists must be wearing their own designs."

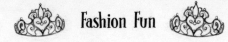

The photographer went over to speak with his assistants.

"Oh no!" said Lena, wringing water out of her shirt. "I'll never win the scholarship now. If I can't do the photo shoot, I'll be eliminated from the competition."

"Maybe we can help you," Mia said softly. She glanced down at her pendant and saw that it was glowing.

"It's no good," said Lena, shaking her head in despair. "Nothing can help."

Charlotte caught Mia's eye and nodded. "Except for magic."

Mia and Charlotte put their shining pendants together, forming a heart. "I wish Lena looked perfect for her photo shoot!"

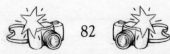

said Mia. There was a bright flash of light and suddenly Lena's clothes were dry. Her hair now fell in soft waves and she was even wearing a bit of sparkly eye shadow and lip gloss.

"How did you—" said Lena, looking down at her clothes in astonishment.

There was no time to explain. Jean-Pierre came over to Lena and said, "I've had a new idea for your photo. I'm going to photograph you over there." He pointed at the carousel nearby. "What do you think?"

"Um, great," said Lena.

Jean-Pierre clapped his hands. "Come along, everyone!" he called out.

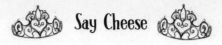

The photographer's assistants picked up all the equipment and headed over to the carousel. As soon as they were out of earshot, Lena turned to Mia, her eyes wide. "How did you do that?" she whispered.

"We told you already," said Mia. "Magic!"

"Mia and I are training to become Secret Princesses," Charlotte explained. "Our necklaces let us use magic to make three little wishes."

"We can use them to help grant your big wish of going to fashion school," added Mia.

"But that's impossible," said Lena. "Magic isn't real."

"Don't you think it's weird that Jean-Pierre didn't say anything about the fact

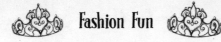

that your clothes were dry all of a sudden?" said Charlotte.

Lena thought about it. "I suppose that *is* kind of odd," she said slowly.

"It's because of the magic," said Mia. "That's how it works. Only the person who we're helping notices."

"Why haven't I ever heard of Secret Princesses before?" Lena asked them, still a bit confused.

"Because they're a secret," Charlotte said with a wink.

"So please don't tell anyone about us," added Mia.

"I won't, I promise," said Lena.

Jean-Pierre and his assistants set up their

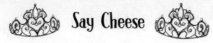

equipment by the carousel. "Sit on this red horse," he instructed Lena.

Lena climbed up on the carousel horse.

"Wind, please," called Jean-Pierre, snapping his fingers. An assistant hurried over with a fan and aimed it at Lena. Her long hair blew back, making it look like the carousel was moving round.

"Cool," said Mia. "I always wondered how they did that in photographs."

"OK, Lena," said Jean-Pierre. "Say cheese. Or as you're in France, you could say *fromage.*"

"Er, *fromage,*" said Lena. She caught Mia's eye and started to giggle. A big smile lit up her face.

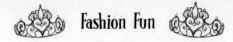
"Perfect!" cried Jean-Pierre, snapping away. "Well done, everyone," he said, packing up his camera. "Now, I think we all deserve a ride on the carousel!"

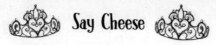
The assistants and other finalists clambered on to the carousel, laughing and chatting. Lena beckoned Mia and Charlotte to join her on the carousel.

"Are you sure it's OK?" asked Mia, climbing up.

"It's the least I can do after you two helped me out," said Lena. "The photo shoot went really well, thanks to you."

Charlotte got on to a pure white horse. "This one reminds me of Snowdrop," she said to Mia, remembering the time they had ridden Princess Ella's magical horses at Wishing Star Palace palace.

Mia climbed on to a grey horse with a jewelled harness and a silky purple tail.

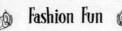

Jolly music started playing and they soared up and down on their wooden horses.

When the ride was over, an elegant woman with long red hair and a cape called the finalists over to her. "Lena, Ellie and Abby," she said, "It's time for the next stage of the competition."

"Who's that?" whispered Mia.

"That's Lola Winters," Lena whispered back. "She's the editor of *Teen Style* magazine."

"Your next task," the editor told them, "will be to design a ballgown."

"Ooh!" squealed Abby, the girl in the silver jumpsuit. She and Ellie, the girl in the tutu, chattered excitedly.

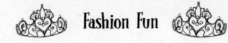

"Ahem!" said Lola, to get their attention. "Your gown should be inspired by Paris. The judges will be looking for creativity so don't just stick to traditional fabrics." Lola held her arms wide. "Look for inspiration all around you!"

Lena held up her hand. "Er, excuse me. Where do we make our gowns?"

Lola gave a throaty laugh. "Oh, and I'm forgetting the most exciting detail! One of the judges, the fashion designer C.C. Grande, is very kindly letting you three use her studio."

"Wow!" Lena whispered to Charlotte and Mia excitedly. "C.C. Grande is my favourite designer ever!"

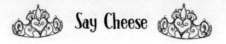
Lola handed each of the finalists an envelope. "Inside you'll find some money to buy all the materials you need, and the studio's address." she told them. "It's easy to find – it's near the Eiffel Tower."

As the contestants chattered nervously, Lola glanced at the gold watch on her wrist.

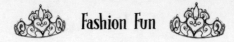
"We want to see how well you can design under pressure. You only have four hours to complete this task – starting ... NOW!"

CHAPTER SIX
The Market

Mia and Charlotte exchanged anxious looks. Four hours didn't sound like much time to make a ballgown! From the looks on the three finalists' faces, it looked like they were worried too.

"Good luck!" Lena called to the other two finalists, as they hurried off in different directions. She turned to Mia and

 95

Charlotte. "I've never made a ballgown before," she said, biting her lip anxiously. "I don't know where to start."

"Why don't you start by going shopping?" suggested Mia. "After all, you can't make a dress without materials."

"Good thinking," said Lena. "Do you two want to come with me?"

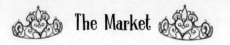

"*Oui!*" said Mia. "That's French for yes."

Charlotte giggled. "I thought you were saying you needed a wee!" She pointed to a sign for a market. "Should we head there?"

"*Oui!*" Lena and Mia said together.

They hurried through the streets and soon reached a bustling market. The cobbled street was lined with cafes and shops.

Shoppers crowded around stalls selling fruit and vegetables and other tasty things.

"Mmm! Something smells nice," said Mia, sniffing the air. The sweet scent was coming from a flower stall selling all kinds of beautiful flowers.

"These are gorgeous," said Charlotte, burying her nose in a bouquet of lilies.

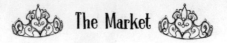

"Could you make a dress out of flower petals?" wondered Charlotte.

"Oh yes!" said Mia. "You could use red, white and blue flowers – like the colours of the French flag."

"Hmm," said Lena. "The petals might wilt by the time I sew them on to a dress."

"I guess we'll have to keep looking then," said Charlotte.

They passed a newsstand with racks of magazines and newspapers. Lena pulled a fashion magazine off the shelf and leafed through the pages.

"Look," she said, showing the girls an ad for a fabulous purple dress. It had a sparkling beaded bodice. The skirt was short

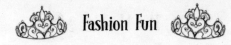
at the front but had a long train of silky ruffles at the back. "C.C. Grande designed this. Isn't it amazing?"

"It's beautiful," said Charlotte.

"She's my hero," Lena told them. "I can't believe get to go to her studio and design there. She studied at the Central Fashion Academy, where I want to go. Oh, I hope this competition goes well!"

Mia glanced at Lena. She was staring at the dress longingly, the way Charlotte looked at Princess Alice when she was performing on stage. This really was her dream.

"I'm sure you will," said Mia, squeezing Lena's hand reassuringly.

"Not if I can't think of an idea for my ballgown," said Lena, sighing and putting the magazine back.

"Hey! What's black and white and red all over?" asked Charlotte.

"I don't know," said Lena, shrugging.

"A newspaper," Charlotte said. "Get it?

It's *read* all over!"

Lena smiled and so did Mia. It was a terrible joke, but Mia was glad Charlotte had cheered Lena up. It had given her an idea, too.

"Maybe you could use newspapers to make your gown," Mia suggested. She wrapped a newspaper around her like a skirt and twirled around.

"You could even make a matching hat," said Charlotte, putting a newspaper on her head and

striking a funny pose.

"No," said Lena, shaking her head. "If it got wet it would be ruined."

As Mia put the newspaper back on the rack, the back of her neck prickled. She had the strangest sensation that she was being watched. She looked around quickly, but everyone she saw was busy shopping. Suddenly Mia wished that she already had her magic sapphire ring – then she'd know if there was danger around.

The next stall was selling fabric. Lena browsed through rolls of different materials, rubbing the cloth between her fingers to feel the textures. There were simple cottons and calicos, and fancy silks and satins.

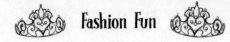
As Lena looked for the perfect fabric, Mia couldn't shake the feeling that someone was watching them. Looking up, she caught a glimpse of someone staring at them from across the street. The person was wearing a trench coat, a beret and dark glasses.

"I think someone might be following us," Mia said, nudging Charlotte.

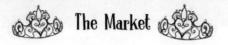

"Hmmm?" said Charlotte, who was stroking some fluffy fake fur. "I haven't noticed anyone."

"Over there," said Mia, pointing across the street. But the person ducked into a cheese shop.

"It's probably because we're talking in a different language," said Charlotte, unconcerned.

"I think I'll get some of this," Lena said, holding up some shimmering white fabric. "Even though I still don't have an idea for my balldress."

"Where to now?" asked Charlotte once Lena had paid for the fabric. "Should we head to the studio?"

Lena frowned. "I don't want to turn up without an idea," she said. "Lola said that inspiration is all around us. So why – oh why – can't I think of an idea?" She looked as if she was about to cry.

Mia scanned the busy market street desperately. Her eyes fell on a café with a beautiful display of pastries and chocolates in the window.

"Let's take a break in there," she said. "Studies show that chocolate helps you think."

"Really?" asked Lena.

"No," said Mia, smiling. "I made that up. But chocolate always cheers me up – and I'm starving!"

As they walked to the café, Charlotte whispered to Mia, "Should we wish for Lena to have a good idea?"

Mia shook her head. "I don't think so," she whispered back. "Lena has plenty of good ideas. I'm sure she'll think of one."

Soon, I hope, she added silently. There were only three hours left now.

A bell tinkled as they went into the café and sat down at a table.

"It all looks so yummy," said Mia, her mouth watering. There were rows of berry-topped tarts, thick cream slices and dainty chocolate cakes.

In the end, they all ordered hot chocolate and éclairs oozing cream. As they ate their delicious pastries, Mia gazed at the display. There were pyramids of pretty pastel macaroons and towers of chocolates with foil wrappers every colour of the rainbow. The wrappers twinkled in the sunlight streaming through the window.

"They look like jewels," Mia said.

Lena's face suddenly lit up. "Mia, you're a genius!" she exclaimed.

"What do you mean?" Mia asked her.

"They *do* look like jewels. Maybe I could use them to decorate my ballgown!" Lena said. She started sketching a design on the back of a paper napkin.

Mia and Charlotte smiled at each other. Lena was excited now that she had an idea! They watched, fascinated, as Lena's design took shape. The ballgown had a full, billowing skirt and a heart-shaped neckline.

"That's so pretty," said Charlotte.

"It will be even prettier when it's sparkling with chocolate jewels," said Lena happily.

She hurried to the counter and bought lots and lots of chocolates, using up all of the money she had left.

Clutching the bag in one hand and her drawing in other, Lena said, "Come on! Let's hurry to C.C. Grande's studio. I can't wait to get started!"

But as they stepped out of the café, Hex jumped out and whacked Lena with a long, thin loaf of bread.

"Hey!" Lena yelped. She was so startled she dropped her bag.

Hex snatched the bag. "Ha ha!" he jeered, waving it in the air. "You can't make your dress without these! Now you'll lose the contest!"

Hex scurried away, but Charlotte caught up to him easily. But before she could stop him,

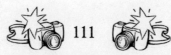

Hex flung the bag across the street.

The person in the trenchcoat, sunglasses and beret caught it and stood there, frozen.

"I knew someone was following us!" gasped Mia.

"Run, you silly girl!" shrieked Hex. "Run!"

As the person sprinted away, the beret flew off, revealing short black hair.

"It's Jinx!" shouted Charlotte. "Don't let her get away!"

"Stop, thief!" yelled Mia.

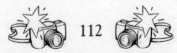

CHAPTER SEVEN
A Sticky Situation

Mia, Charlotte and Lena chased after Jinx.
They ran down the busy market street,
dodging shoppers and skirting around
poodles on leads.

"We can't let her get away!" said Lena,
panting. "I don't have any money left to
buy more chocolates!"

"Don't worry, Lena," shouted Charlotte.

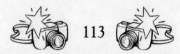

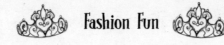
"We'll catch her!"

But Jinx was a lot faster than Hex. They reached the end of the street and looked around. They couldn't see her anywhere.

"There she is!" cried Mia. She pointed across a busy road. Jinx was running up the steps leading to a big museum.

"After her!" said Charlotte.

The girls dashed into the museum and saw Jinx run into a long room full of all kinds of paintings.

They chased her through the gallery, which was packed with tourists admiring the famous works of art.

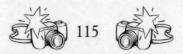

"Stop!" cried a museum guard, but the
girls ignored him and carried on running.
They couldn't let Jinx out of their sight!

Jinx darted from one room to another,
trying to shake off her pursuers, but the girls
stayed close on her trail. Finally, they ran
into a small room at the end of a corridor.

"Where's she gone?" said Mia, slowing
to a halt. There was only one way out of
the room.

"There she is!" shouted Charlotte.

Jinx was hiding behind a marble statue
of an ancient goddess, Lena's bag behind
her back.

"Give Lena back her chocolates right
now!" Charlotte demanded.

Jinx shook her head. "I'll get in big trouble," she said, cowering in fright.

"You don't have a choice," said Mia. "We've got you cornered."

Jinx dropped the bag and slid it across the floor. As Lena darted forward to grab it, Jinx ran off, sobbing.

"Who is that girl?" Lena asked Mia and Charlotte. "Why does she keep doing mean things to me?"

"Her name is Jinx," said Charlotte. "She and the man who snatched your bag work for someone called Princess Poison."

"I thought the princesses were good!" exclaimed Lena.

"Not that one," said Mia, shaking her head. "She tries to spoil wishes instead of granting them." She looked up at a clock and gasped. "And she'll succeed if we don't hurry. There's not much time left – you need to start making your dress!"

They tried to retrace their steps, but the museum was like a maze. There were rooms and rooms filled with artworks – and they all looked the same.

"I think we were just in here," Charlotte

said, as they wandered into a room filled with paintings of kinds and queens. "I remember that painting – that old king looks kind of like my softball coach."

"Oh, no!" wailed Lena. "We're lost! I'm never going to have enough time to make my ballgown!"

"Should we use one of our wishes?" Charlotte asked Mia.

"I've got a better idea," said Mia, spotting a map of the museum.

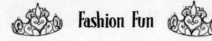
She ran to the map and studied it quickly and then said, "Follow me!"

As Mia led her friends through the museum, she thought of the princesses whose portraits Princess Poison had cursed. "I really hope Sylvie, Sophie, Cara and Kiko are OK," she murmured to Charlotte.

"I was thinking the same thing," said

Charlotte. "Do you think they're still at the Hexagon?"

"I'm not sure," said Mia. "But one thing's certain – Princess Poison is definitely trying to spoil Lena's wish."

"Jinx doesn't seem very happy about it, though," said Charlotte.

"I know," said Mia. "It's really strange. I wonder why she's working for her."

At last, they found their way out of the museum. Mia blinked as her eyes adjusted to the bright sunlight. "How do we get to the studio?" she asked.

"Lola said it was near the Eiffel Tower," said Lena. "So let's head that way." The tower was very tall so it was easy to see.

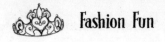
The girls started jogging in that direction, not wanting to lose any more time.

They soon found the street where C.C. Grande's studio was located.

"Here it is!" cried Lena as they reached a door with C.C. Grande's logo in elegant gold letters.

They knocked and entered. Inside the busy studio, the other two finalists were already hard at work on their ballgowns.

Ellie, the girl in the tutu, was making a
dress out of silk scarves. A sewing machine
whirred as she stitched them on to the waist
to make floaty layers.

"That's really pretty," said Mia.

"So's that," said Charlotte, pointing on
the dress that Abby, the finalist with the
silver jumpsuit, was making. She was sewing
brightly coloured feathers on to a long,
slinky ballgown.

Lena found a work bench and quickly
got to work. Glancing at her sketch on the
napkin, she quickly drew a paper pattern.
Using the pattern, she cut the white fabric
into pieces and pinned them into position.
Then she started stitching the pieces
together with a sewing machine. The
ballgown was starting to take shape!

"Wow!" said Mia. "She's really fast!"

Lena hung the white dress on a
mannequin, then started making
adjustments – pinning the waist to tighten
it and raising the hem a few inches.

Soon the gown looked just like the sketch
Lena had drawn in the café. There was a
long, full skirt and a fitted heart-shaped

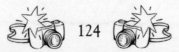

neckline with thin, spaghetti straps.

"Now for the jewels," Lena said, grinning. Using fabric glue, she started sticking chocolates on to the dress. She arranged them by colour, so they shimmered like a rainbow. Mia and Charlotte helped out by sorting the chocolates by colour and handing Lena the ones she needed.

"Ten minutes left, girls," said Lola, coming into the studio to check how the three finalists were getting on.

"I need some more pink ones," said Lena, a note of panic in her voice.

"Here you go," said Mia, quickly handing her some more of the chocolates in the pink foil wrappers.

"It's looking amazing," Charlotte
reassured Lena.

Lena stuck on one last chocolate jewel
and took a step back to look at her creation.
"What do you think?" she asked Mia and
Charlotte nervously.

"Gorgeous," said Charlotte. The foil
chocolate wrappers glittered like sequins,
making the whole dress sparkle.

"It's fit for a princess," said Mia.

"Good thing I'm here, then," said Princess
Poison from across the room.

Mia gasped as she heard the familiar
voice. She turned to see Princess Poison
smirking at the girls. Nobody but Mia,
Charlotte and Lena noticed her arrival.

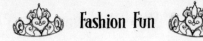
Ellie and Abby were busy putting the finishing touches on their dresses.

"Mia didn't mean *you*," Charlotte said, glaring at Princess Poison.

Princess Poison circled the mannequin, running her long nails over the ballgown. "Very nice," she drawled. "But I'm not sure it's right for this sunny weather." Fanning herself, she asked, "Is anyone else feeling rather … hot?"

Pointing her wand at Lena's gown, Princess Poison hissed out a spell:

**"Melt these chocolates, sweet and brown,
Wreck the gown and make her frown!"**

There was a flash of green light and all of
the chocolates on Lena's ballgown melted.
Sticky, brown chocolate dripped out of the
foil wrappers, spilling on to the white fabric.
The beautiful ballgown was ruined!

"Face it, girls," sneered Princess Poison. "You're outnumbered. I've got two helpers now, so you'll never stop me!"

She waved her wand again and vanished in a flash of green light.

"My gown!" wailed Lena. "She's completely ruined it! I'll never win a scholarship to fashion school now!"

"One minute!" came Lola's voice, reminding the finalists that their time was nearly up.

Mia looked at Charlotte and nodded. There was only one thing to do. It was time to make another wish!

CHAPTER EIGHT
A Special Tour

Mia and Charlotte held their glowing
pendants together, forming a heart. "I wish
for Lena's dress to be fixed," said Mia.

There was a flash of light and the
ballgown went back to how it had looked
before Princess Poison cast her nasty spell.
But now it had accessories, too! There was
a hat made out of a heart-shaped box of

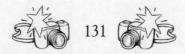

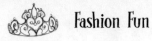

chocolates and a handbag that looked just like an éclair!

Lena gasped, her hands flying to her mouth. Astounded, she turned to the girls and said, "Thank you so much. You saved me again."

"No problem," said Charlotte. "We couldn't let Princess Poison get away with that."

"So that was Princess Poison?" Lena asked them.

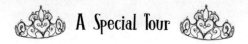

"Yes," said Mia. "And I doubt we've seen the last of her."

Before Mia could say anything more, Lola came back and clapped her hands. "Time's up, girls," she told the finalists. "Now I'd like to introduce you to the person who has very kindly let you use her studio. Please welcome C.C. Grande!"

A young woman with her hair in twists, wearing a bold orange dress, came into the room. She beamed at the finalists.

Mia and Charlotte gasped as they recognised her. It was Princess Cara!

"I had no idea Cara was C.C. Grande," Mia whispered to Charlotte.

"Or that she was famous," said Charlotte.

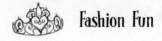
Cara walked around the studio, chatting to the finalists and looking at their ballgowns. Finally it was Lena's turn

"Your dress looks good enough to eat," Cara said, smiling kindly at Lena. "Where did you get the idea?" she asked.

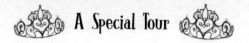

"I was in a café with my friends," Lena said, nodding at Mia and Charlotte. "And we realised that the chocolates looked just like jewels."

"Great work!" Cara said encouragingly. She started walking over to Lola. But the girls couldn't let her go without trying to help her remember!

"You know who else would like this dress," Charlotte said as she raced after Cara. "Sylvie. *Princess* Sylvie," she said meaningfully.

She stared at Cara, willing her to understand, but she just looked at Charlotte blankly. Charlotte turned to Mia for help.

"That's right," said Mia. "Everyone at

Wishing Star Palace loves Princess Sylvie's magical cakes."

Cara laughed. "Well, I love cake," she said. "But I'm afraid I don't know anything about magic."

"You do," insisted Mia. "Look!" She showed Cara her half-heart pendant. "We've got magic pendants just like yours." She pointed to the thimble-shaped necklace around Cara's neck. "We can do magic to grant wishes!"

"Magic jewellery! Now that's a brilliant idea," said Princess Cara, glancing down at the thimble pendant on her own magic necklace. "I'm sure everyone would want to buy it!"

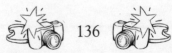

Mia looked at Charlotte and shook her head sadly. Princess Cara didn't understand anything they were telling her. Princess Poison's curse had made her forget everything about being a Secret Princess.

"Would you girls like to see some jewellery from my latest collection?" Cara asked them. "It isn't magical, but I think you'll like it."

"Ooh, yes, please," Lena said excitedly.

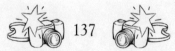

She was eager to spend as much time as possible with the designer.

Cara led them out of the workroom into a smaller room, with fashion sketches and fabric samples pinned to the walls. There were boxes of buttons and beads, rolls of fabric and mannequins wearing half-finished clothing.

"This is my office," Cara said. "It's where I work on all my newest designs." She pulled open a drawer and took out some chunky bracelets and beaded necklaces. "My family is from Sierra Leone, originally," Cara explained. "So these pieces are inspired by traditional Sierra Leonean designs."

"They're beautiful," said Lena, trying on

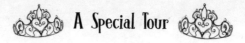

one of the bracelets.

Cara led them round to her drawing table, where there was a sketch of a suit.

"Hmm," said Cara, frowning at the drawing. "I'm still not happy with this."

"Can I try something?" Lena asked shyly.

"Of course," said Cara, handing her a pencil.

Lena quickly drew a few lines. The suit jacket now had a high collar and big, bold buttons. The skirt was tight down to the knee, then flared out.

"I love it!" said Cara. "Thanks for your help, Lena!"

Lena's cheeks flushed pink at Cara's praise. "Thanks, C.C." she said.

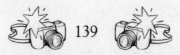

"Call me Cara," said Cara, smiling. "My middle name is Catherine – that's what C.C. stands for. Let me take you to see the showroom now," Cara went on. She led them down a hallway and through a door.

"Wow!" said Charlotte. The showroom had enormous vases full of exotic flowers and huge mirrors everywhere. Beautiful dresses, shirts, trousers and jackets, all designed by Cara, hung from the clothes rails. In the middle of the room stood a mannequin wearing the purple dress that Lena had shown them in the fashion magazine. The bodice glittered with hundreds and hundreds of tiny crystal beads and the silk ruffles on the skirt's long train

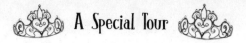

looked like a flowing waterfall. It was even more gorgeous than it had looked in the magazine.

"I love this dress so much," said Lena, running her hand over the fabric.

"You can take it off the mannequin if you want to have a closer look," said Cara.

"Are you sure?" asked Lena.

"Of course," said Cara.

Lena carefully took the dress off the mannequin. "Wow," she said, as she examined the gown in awe. "It must have taken so long to sew all the beads on!"

As Lena admired Cara's work, a bell tinkled and two familiar people came in. Mia groaned as she saw who it was.

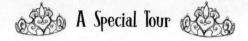

Princess Poison smirked at the girls, while Jinx squirmed uncomfortably.

"Hello," Cara greeted them. "How can I help you?"

Mia gasped. Cara didn't recognise Princess Poison!

"We're looking for something special to wear to the *Teen Style* fashion show tonight," Princess Poison said.

"What a coincidence!" exclaimed Cara. "The finalists have been working in my studio today."

"Oh, is that so?" drawled Princess Poison with a smug smile. "I had no idea." She wandered around the showroom,

pretending to be interested in the clothing. "Hmm," she said. "I don't see anything quite right. Do you have anything else you could show us?"

"Let me check," said Cara. "I'll be right back." She left the showroom.

"That's such a lovely frock," said Princess Poison. She pulled out her wand,

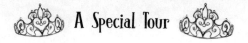

pointed it at the dress Lena was holding and snarled:

**"Sparkling beads, fall off that dress.
Spill all over and make a mess!"**

"No!" cried Charlotte, running over to try and grab Princess Poison's wand. But it was too late. A bolt of bad green magic hit the dress Lena was holding. Hundreds of crystal beads flew off the dress and scattered all over the shop floor like glittering confetti.

"Tut tut!" said Princess Poison. "That dress is worth a fortune. C.C. Grande won't be very impressed when she discovers that you've ruined it!"

She snapped her fingers and Jinx came

hurrying over to her side.

"I'm sure I won't see you at the fashion show," Princess Poison said to Lena. "Because you'll surely be kicked out of the competition now. Oh, what a pity!"

Then she swept out of the showroom, slamming the door behind her.

CHAPTER NINE
Model Behaviour

"Oh no!" said Lena, looking down at the ruined purple gown in despair. "I've got to try and fix it!" She took a step and slipped on the tiny crystal beads that had rolled all over the floor.

"Help!" she yelped, flailing her arms to try and stay upright. As she skidded across the shop floor, Lena grabbed a mannequin to steady herself. The mannequin toppled over

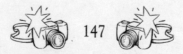

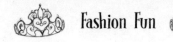

and Lena fell on top of it.

Charlotte darted forward to help Lena up, but she slipped on the beads too!

"Waaaa!" Charlotte went flying, her arms spinning like a windmill. She bumped into a huge vase of orchids. CRASH! The vase fell

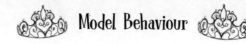

to the floor and shattered. Water from the vase pooled on the floor and tiny shards of glass scattered everywhere.

"Charlotte!" gasped Mia. She ran over to help her friends but her feet flew out from under her. She grabbed hold of a clothes rail

to steady herself and it collapsed. Dresses,
trousers and shirts fell off their hangers and
on to the wet floor.

"This is a disaster!" wailed Lena. "The
showroom's a mess! I'll never be able to pay
for all this damage!"

Mia glanced down at her pendant. It was
still glowing faintly. She knew they needed
to use their last wish now, or Lena would
never get a chance to win the scholarship.
She crawled over the floor carefully,
avoiding the sharp pieces of glass.

"Quick, Charlotte!" she said. "Let's make
a wish!"

They put their pendants together. "I
wish the purple dress and Cara's showroom

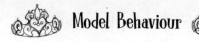

were all back to normal," Charlotte said.

There was a flash of light and the showroom was back to how Cara had left it. The mannequin was upright, clothes were hanging up neatly again, the floor was dry and the vase was all in one piece. Most importantly of all, the crystal beads were back on the purple dress.

It was just in time. Cara came back into
the shop holding two dresses.

"Where did the tall lady and the girl go?"
she asked.

"Um, they left," said Charlotte.

"Never mind," said Cara, hanging the two
dresses on a clothes rail. "They didn't seem
like much fun."

If only you knew, Mia thought.

"We'd better get back to the others," Cara
said. "It's nearly time for the fashion show."

They returned to the studio where the
other finalists were waiting with their
parents.

"The fashion show is taking place at
a palace," Lola told the three finalists.

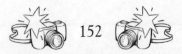

"Your clothes are there already."

Outside, a long, black limousine was waiting for them! Ellie and Abby followed Lola and Cara into the limousine.

Lena hesitated. "Can my friends come too?" she asked Lola.

"Of course," the editor said, patting the seat. "There's plenty of room in here."

"Wow!" said Mia, stepping into the limo. She'd never been in such a big car! Long, leather seats stretched the entire length of the limo. There was even a bar serving fizzy drinks!

As the girls sipped glasses of lemonade, Lena explained the fashion show to them. "It's the most important part of the

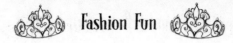

competition. We each get to show six different outfits that we've designed. Famous models are going to wear them!"

Soon they arrived outside a very grand palace in the centre of Paris.

"What do you think, girls?" asked Cara.

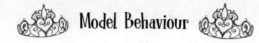

"It's almost as beautiful as Wishing Star Palace," said Mia, trying her best to remind Cara again.

But Cara smiled at her, looking puzzled.

Inside the palace, the finalists were introduced to the models who would be wearing their clothes in the fashion show.

"Ava will be modelling your clothes, Lena," said Lola.

Ava was very tall and very beautiful, with huge brown eyes and long, glossy hair. She smiled at Lena and went over to try on the outfits. Lena made some last-minute adjustments to make sure that her clothes fitted the model perfectly.

"These are great!" Ava said to Lena.

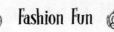

"I'd better go and get my hair and make-
done, so I look as good as the outfits!" she
added, changing back into her own clothes
when the fitting session was over.

"Phew!" said Lena, when she was alone
with Mia and Charlotte. "I'm so relieved
that the clothes fit Ava."

"Are you sure they fit her?" asked a
chillingly familiar voice. "I think you might
have got the size wrong."

The girls turned around and saw Princess
Poison, standing with Jinx and Hex on
either side of her.

Princess Poison narrowed her eyes and
pointed her wand at Lena's clothes for the
fashion show.

"Shrink these clothes, make them small,
The perfect size to fit a doll!"

A stream of green light poured out of Princess Poison's wand and hit the clothes. They instantly started shrinking.

"No!" gasped Lena. Her outfits were getting smaller and smaller and smaller …

Suddenly, Jinx lost her balance and bumped into Princess Poison, jostling her arm. The wand pointed away from Lena's clothing and the bad green magic hit Hex instead!

"Hey!" he shrieked as his suit suddenly started shrinking. *Pop! Pop!* Buttons flew off his shirt and his trousers looked like shorts.

Every seam was straining and Hex looked ready to burst out of his clothes.

Charlotte couldn't help giggling. She caught Jinx's eye, and was pretty sure she was trying hard not to laugh too.

"You clumsy girl!" Princess Poison yelled

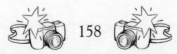

at Jinx. "You interrupted my spell!"

"I think Jinx did that on purpose,"
Charlotte whispered to Mia.

"What's going on here?" asked Cara,
joining them. She looked at Princess Poison
suspiciously. "I don't think you should be
backstage."

"We were just going," said Princess
Poison. She grabbed Jinx's arm and swept
her away. Hex trailed after them, trying
to pull his too-small shirt over his bulging
tummy.

Lola hurried backstage. "Five minutes
until show time, girls!" she told the finalists.

"Good luck, Lena," Cara said, following
Lola out into the audience.

Ava came back. Her dark hair had been styled into a sleek bun. She was wearing shimmery eye shadow and bright red lipstick.

The model tried to put on the first outfit – a gorgeous blue dress with silk butterflies sewn all over it. But she couldn't even pull it over her knees!

She tried to change into a

glittery pink dress but she couldn't get that over her head either.

Jinx might have interupted Princess Poison's spell before the outfits could become dolls' clothes, but they had still shrunk much smaller than before.

"I'm really sorry," the model said, handing the dress back to Lena. "But these clothes are completely the wrong size. They're like children's clothes."

"What am I going to do?" said Lena. "I don't have a hope of winning if my clothes aren't in the fashion show."

Mia held up the butterfly dress sadly. "I'm so sorry," she said. "We don't have any wishes left to help you."

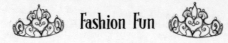
Lena's eyes suddenly lit up. "You might still be able to help me, though … " she said hopefully.

"What do you mean?" asked Mia.

Lena held the glittery dress up to Charlotte. "You heard Ava – they're kid-sized!" she said. "Would you please model them for me in the fashion show?"

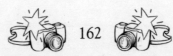

CHAPTER TEN

Dress for Success

"But we're not models!" Mia said. She didn't really like being the centre of attention, so the idea of being on stage with everyone looking at her made her tummy feel funny!

"No," said Lena, "But all of the real models are too tall to wear my clothes now."

"Come on, Mia!" Charlotte said. "We just need to wear the clothes and walk around."

"I don't know," said Mia nervously. "I might trip up …"

Charlotte took Mia's hand. "We'll do it together," she said. "Every step of the way."

"Please," Lena begged them. "You two are my only hope."

Mia gulped. "Of course," she said. "We promised to help grant your wish. "

Charlotte hugged her. "You're being really brave," she whispered in Mia's ear.

Lola hurried backstage again, her cape billowing out behind her. "One minute until the show starts!" she said. "Good luck, everyone!"

Mia and Charlotte quickly put on their first outfits.

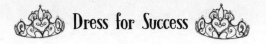

"You guys look great," said Lena. Mia
was wearing a long dress with a ruffly top.
Charlotte wore a black and white striped
cheerleader skirt with a polka dotted top.

"Ladies and gentlemen, welcome to the
Teen Style Fashion Show," announced

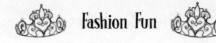

Lola. Loud rock music started playing.

"Here goes," said Mia, stepping out on to the catwalk with Charlotte.

Music boomed and cameras flashed as photographers snapped pictures of them. The audience was sitting along both sides of the catwalk, looking up at the models

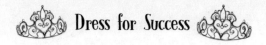

as they strutted up and down. At the end
of the catwalk sat the three judges – Lola,
Cara and Jean-Pierre the photographer.

"Turn around," Charlotte whispered
to Mia when they reached the end of
the catwalk. They both twirled and the
audience clapped politely.

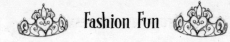
"Phew!" said Mia, when they were backstage again. "I didn't trip."

"You were amazing," Charlotte told her.

"Hurry and get changed," said Lena, handing them their next outfits.

Mia quickly put on a red satin jumpsuit embroidered with green dragons. Charlotte wore a neon yellow track suit with lots of

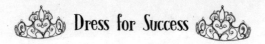
hot-pink zippers. Then they were off again,
striding down the catwalk. At the end,
Mia struck a pose while Charlotte turned a
cartwheel then did the splits.

"Woo hoo!" everyone cheered.

Well, not quite everyone. Mia spotted
Princess Poison
scowling in
the front row
audience, her
arms crossed over
her chest. She was
wearing an enormous pair
of sunglasses and looking
very cross. Next to her,
Jinx was clapping.

Just then, Princess Poison noticed and
jabbed Jinx with a bony elbow.

"This is actually
kind of fun," Mia
admitted as she
and Charlotte
changed into
their final
outfits. Mia
zipped up the
swishy butterfly
dress. Charlotte
slipped on the glittery
pink dress.

"You two are naturals,"
said Ava, as Charlotte and Mia got ready to

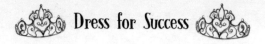
be models one last time.

The girls strode down the catwalk hand-in-hand. When they got to the end, Charlotte twirled Mia around. The audience whooped.

At the end of the show, Lola called all the models and finalists back on to the catwalk to take a bow. "The judges have reached a decision," she announced. "The winner of this year's young designer competition is … Lena Kowalski!"

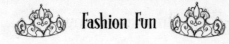
"You did it!" cried Charlotte, as Mia jumped up and down with excitement.

"I can't believe it," Lena said, tears of joy streaming down her cheeks. "I'm actually

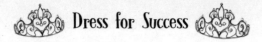
going to go to fashion school!"

"Lena, come and take a victory walk down the catwalk," Lola called.

"You two come with me," said Lena, holding out her hands to Mia and Charlotte. "I couldn't have done it without you both. My wish has come true!"

They all walked down the catwalk together, waving to the audience. At the end of the catwalk, Mia twirled and the silk butterflies on her dress magically came to life, fluttering into the air.

"Ooooh!" gasped the audience.

Then Charlotte twirled, and her glittery skirt created rainbow-coloured sparkles.

"Aaaaah!" sighed the audience.

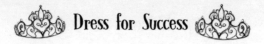

Mia grinned at Charlotte, who winked at her. They both knew the magic was because Lena's wish had been granted.

Mia saw Princess Poison dragging Jinx along a row of seats, a furious look on her face. Jinx glanced back over her shoulder longingly, like she was trying to catch one last glimpse of the fashion show. Mia almost felt sorry for Jinx, despite what she'd done to Lena.

Backstage, Cara came over and kissed Lena on each cheek. "Congratulations! I learned so much at the Central Fashion Academy," she told her. "I know you'll love studying there!"

"I can't wait to go," Lena said happily.

"My mum will be so proud of me."

"I know the scholarship is your prize," said Cara, "But I'd like to give you something else – the purple dress from my showroom."

"But … but … it's worth so much money," Lena stammered.

"You love it so much," said Cara. "I really

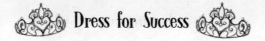
wish you could have it."

As she spoke, her necklace glowed and suddenly Lena was holding the purple beaded dress!

"You see, you *are* a Secret Princess!" Charlotte exclaimed.

Stunned, Cara turned to Mia and Charlotte. "I'm really sorry I didn't believe what you two have been trying to tell me," she said. "I still don't understand it. But there's no other way to explain what just happened – not to mention the butterflies and sparkles. It must be magic!"

"It will make sense soon," Mia reassured Cara. "I promise." She turned to Charlotte. "We need to take Cara to Wishing Star

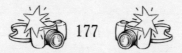

Palace to break Princess Poison's curse."

"But how?" asked Charlotte.

There was another flash of light. Mia glanced down and saw that she and Charlotte were now wearing their ruby slippers! "We've got to go," she told Lena.

Lena hugged them both. "Thank you so much for your help."

"Good luck at fashion school," Charlotte said. "I'll look out for your clothes!"

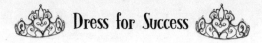

"Wait! I have something for you," said Lena. She gave Mia a sketch of the butterfly outfit, and Charlotte a sketch of the glittery pink dress.

"Thank you!" said Mia. "It's gorgeous."

"It will remind me of our adventure!" Charlotte said.

"Will you come with us?" Mia asked Cara, holding out her hand.

Cara nodded and they all held hands. Mia and Charlotte clicked the heels of their ruby slippers together and said, "Wishing Star Palace!"

Magic swept them away and they landed back at Wishing Star Palace, wearing their princess dresses and tiaras.

Has Princess Poison's curse been broken?
Mia wondered.

"Do you know where you are?" Mia asked
Cara nervously.

"Of course I do," said Cara, beaming at
them. "I'm back at Wishing Star Palace,

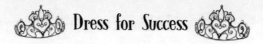
right where a Secret Princess belongs!" She took out her wand. "And there's something I need to do." She touched her wand to Mia's pendant, and then to Charlotte's. A sparking blue sapphire magically appeared on each girl's pendant!

"Thank you for not giving up on me and making me believe in magic again," Cara said to them.

"We'd never give up on a Secret Princess," said Charlotte.

"Never," echoed Mia. She suddenly thought of something and started running up the stairs.

"Where are you going?" Charlotte called.

"Come and see!" Mia shouted back.

Charlotte and Cara followed her up the stairs and along a corridor.

"It's back!" Mia cried. Princess Cara's painting was hanging on the wall of the portrait gallery once more. Bringing Cara back to the palace had brought the portrait back, too!

The other princesses had heard them shouting and came to see what the commotion was about.

"You're back!" squealed Alice in delight, giving Cara a hug.

"All thanks to these two," said Cara. "They broke Princess Poison's curse by getting me to believe in magic and bringing me back to Wishing Star Palace."

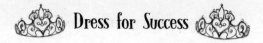
Mia stared at the three empty spaces where Sylvie, Sophie and Kiko's paintings usually hung. She was glad Cara was back, but there were still three other princesses who needed their help.

Alice stroked Mia's arm. "Don't worry," she told her. "They'll soon be back at the palace, too."

"And so will you," Cara added. "To grant more wishes and earn more sapphires."

"But right now, it's time for you to go home," Alice said.

Mia and Charlotte said farewell to the princesses and then they hugged each other.

"*Au revoir!*" Mia told Charlotte happily. "That's goodbye in French."

Cara waved her wand and Mia suddenly found herself back in her empty classroom at school. She grabbed her jacket and hurried outside to the playground, where the other children were still playing cops and robbers.

"Come on, Mia," called her friend Emily. "Help us get the baddies!"

Mia grinned and ran to join the game. She wasn't afraid of baddies. After all, she and Charlotte had just stopped Princess Poison. *And*, Mia thought happily, *we'll do it again soon!*

The End

Join Charlotte and Mia in their next Secret Princesses adventure

Read on for a sneak peek!

Brilliant Bake Off

"Can we get some oranges, Mum?"
Charlotte Williams asked her mother as
they strolled through the bustling market
hand in hand. Charlotte thought the stalls
looked like rainbows, their wooden crates
displaying brightly coloured fruits and
vegetables – from glossy purple aubergines
to ruby-red cherries.

"Of course," said her mum, handing
Charlotte a bag. "Get lots and we can
make juice."

Tucking her brown curls behind her ears,

Charlotte leaned over a crate of oranges and looked for the biggest, juiciest ones she could find. She breathed in their citrus scent. "Mmm," she said. "They smell like sunshine!"

Since moving to California from England, coming to the local market on Saturday morning had become a new tradition for Charlotte's family.

"Get a few peaches, too," said Charlotte's mum. "They look good."

Charlotte added some plump, fuzzy peaches to the bag.

Bored of shopping, Charlotte's six-year-old twin brothers were pretending that they were space knights, using cucumbers as laser swords.

"Give up now!" cried Liam, swinging a cucumber at his twin brother, Harvey.

"Never!" shouted Harvey, blocking the blow with another cucumber.

"Give me those right now or there'll be nothing left for our salad," Charlotte's dad said, interrupting the boys' duel.

"Aw, Dad," complained Harvey, reluctantly handing his father the cucumber. "You're no fun."

"Really?" said dad, raising an eyebrow playfully. "So I guess you don't want to help me make tacos for dinner tonight?"

"Tacos?" said Liam, his face lighting up. "Yum!"

"If you boys find me some avocadoes, we can make guacamole too," said Charlotte's dad, rubbing Harvey's short, curly hair affectionately.

When the twins returned, each holding a knobbly green avocado, Dad paid the farmer for their shopping.

"I think we all deserve a treat," Dad said.

Charlotte grinned at her brothers, her brown eyes sparkling. This was the best part of coming to the market!

Dad led them over to a stall with a mouth-watering display of baked goods. There were gooey brownies, big, chewy cookies and cupcakes topped with swirls of buttercream icing. "You can each choose something," he told the children.

It was hard to decide, but Charlotte finally settled on a brownie. The twins both picked chocolate-chip cookies.

"Anything for you, hon?" Charlotte's dad asked her mum.

"Could I have an English breakfast tea, please?" she replied. Charlotte's dad ordered a tea for himself, too.

Charlotte grinned to herself. Even though her family seemed more American all the time, some things hadn't changed – like her parents still drinking tea!

As she walked through the market nibbling her brownie, Charlotte suddenly thought of Mia, her best friend who lived

in England. Even though they now lived
thousands of miles apart, Mia still sent
Charlotte parcels of home-baked treats. For
Charlotte's last birthday, Mia had baked
Charlotte biscuits shaped like tiaras, stars
and hearts. They tasted delicious, but the
biscuits were more than just a yummy treat
– they were a reminder of the amazing
secret she and Mia shared. They were
training to become Secret Princesses!

Shortly before Charlotte had moved to
California, a family friend called Alice
had given Mia and Charlotte necklaces
with matching half-heart pendants. Alice
had explained that the girls both had the
potential to become Secret Princesses, who

could grant wishes using magic! Best of all,
it meant that Charlotte and Mia could still
see each other at Wishing Star Palace, a
gorgeous castle in the clouds. Training to
become a princess with Mia was the coolest
thing that had ever happened to Charlotte.

Glancing down at her pendant, Charlotte
gasped. It was glowing!

"I'm just going to have a look at that stall
over there," Charlotte told her parents, who
were tasting samples of honey.

Finishing the last bite of her brownie,
she ducked behind some wooden crates.
No time would pass here while she was
having a magical adventure with Mia, so
Charlotte didn't need to worry about her

parents missing her. Holding her half-heart pendant, Charlotte whispered, "I wish I could see Mia."

Golden light streamed out of the pendant, glowing brighter and brighter until it had completely surrounded Charlotte. She felt the light whisking her away from the farmers' market.

WHOOSH!

A moment later, Charlotte landed in the marble entrance hall of Wishing Star Palace. Her denim dungarees and trainers had been magically transformed into a pale pink princess dress and sparkling ruby slippers. Charlotte patted her head, checking that there was a diamond tiara resting on top of her curls. But something was missing …

"Looking for someone?" asked Mia Thompson, grinning as she appeared out of thin air.

Mia was wearing a golden princess dress that matched her long blonde hair and sparkled like her blue eyes. Like Charlotte, she wore the glittering diamond tiara they had earned for completing the first stage of their princess training. On her feet were the ruby slippers they'd earned for finishing the second stage of their training.

"I've found her now," Charlotte said, running over to give her best friend a hug.

"You've been eating chocolate," Mia said,

waggling her finger.

"How did you know?" Charlotte asked.

"Magic," said Mia mysteriously.

"Really?" Charlotte asked, her eyes growing wide in amazement.

"No, silly," Mia said, giggling. "You've still got some around your mouth."

Charlotte laughed and rubbed the chocolate off. "I was at a market with my family," she explained. "You'd love it."

"I wonder where all the princesses are?" asked Mia.

They wandered through the ground floor, peeping into the throne room, the ballroom and the dining room. But the elegant rooms were all empty.

At the bottom of one of the palace's four towers, Charlotte could hear the faint sound of music and laughter coming from far above.

"They must be up there," Charlotte said.

"It sounds like they're having a party!" Mia exclaimed.

"Well then," said Charlotte, holding out her hand to Mia with a smile. "What are we waiting for?"

"We've never been up here before," panted Mia as they climbed up the twisting spiral staircase.

"There are lots of rooms we still haven't explored," Charlotte said. They'd visited the palace many times, but there was always a new place to discover!

As they reached the top of the stairs, a door opened. A princess holding a guitar beamed at them. She had cool red streaks in her strawberry blonde hair.

"Oh, hello! I was just coming to look for you," said Princess Alice. "I suddenly realised that you two have never been up to the Astronomy Tower before."

"We worked out where to go," said Mia.

"Of course you did," said Alice, giving both girls a hug. "Our trainee princesses are brave, kind AND clever!"

Back in the real world, Alice was a pop star. But Charlotte and Mia weren't

star-struck because they had known
Alice for a long time. She had been their
babysitter when they were little, before
she'd won a TV talent show and become
famous.

"Come in," said Alice, ushering them
inside. "We're having a party!"

The girls stepped into a room with a
domed glass ceiling. In the middle of the
room, a huge, gold telescope pointed up
at the sky. A magical model of the solar
system floated in mid-air, with gorgeous
jewelled planets orbiting a shining golden
model of the sun. The room was crowded
with princesses chatting and sipping drinks.

"Wow!" said Charlotte, looking up at the

stars twinkling overhead.

"It's awesome up here, isn't it?" said Alice.

"What are you celebrating?" asked Mia.

"It's a welcome home party," explained Alice. "One of our friends has been away from Wishing Star Palace for a whole year."

Charlotte suddenly noticed a banner stretching across the room. It read *Welcome Back, Princess Luna!* "Let me guess," she said. "Is her name Luna?"

"Yes," Alice replied, squeezing the girls' shoulders fondly. "And she can't wait to meet you!"

Alice led Mia and Charlotte over to a princess in a pearly white gown. Her dark hair was cropped short in a pixie cut and she wore a necklace with a pendant shaped like a crescent moon.

"Luna," said Alice, placing her hand gently on Luna's shoulder. "Can I introduce you to Mia and Charlotte?"

Luna's brown eyes widened in delight. "The new trainees!" she cried. "I've heard so much about you."

Mia blushed and smiled shyly. "It's really nice to meet you," she said politely.

"I love your pendant," said Charlotte.

A Secret Princess's pendant showed her special talent, which was why Alice's necklace had a musical note. Mia and Charlotte's half-heart pendants were very unusual – they showed that the girls had a gift for friendship, which was why they always worked as a pair.

Luna touched her necklace and smiled. "It's shaped like a moon because I'm an astrophysicist."

Charlotte's brow wrinkled in confusion. "An astro-what?"

"I'm a scientist who studies the universe," Luna explained.

"Luna knows everything there is to know about the stars and planets," said Alice. "Now if you'll excuse me, I promised Luna I'd play my new song for her."

Read Brilliant Bake Off to find out what happens next!

Princess Cara's Fashion Tips

Dressing up is so much fun! Here
Princess Cara shares her tips on letting
your inner princess shine through.

- Wear your favourite colour to feel happy and confident
- Accessorise your outfit with some pretty jewellery – why not try a pendant necklace like Charlotte and Mia?
- Add a colourful belt to transform your favourite dress
- Customise old clothes to create a completely new look
- Try out different patterns and colours to see what suits you best
- Don't forget your hair! A hairband will look just like a tiara
- Remember – no outfit is complete without a smile!

Lena's Fashion Fun

Do you have some jeans that are getting old?
Transform them into these gorgeous customised
shorts! Just remember to check with an adult first
and ask for help when cutting.

You will need:

- Jeans
- Scissors
- Needle and thread
- Buttons/beads/bits of material/patches/fabric paint

Instructions:

1) Using some chalk, mark a line along your jeans a couple of centimetres below where you want to cut. This will mean you won't make them too short by accident!

2) Carefully cut along the line you traced. Don't worry if they don't look perfectly even, you can neaten them up.

3) Customise! Sew on some buttons around the pockets, some beads around the hem, make some patches with the material – anything you like!

4) Try on your new shorts and feel like a princess!

♥ # WIN A PRINCESS GOODY BAG ♥

What would you wish for?

Design your own dress and win a Secret Princesses goody bag for you and your best friend!

Charlotte and Mia get to wear beautiful dresses at Wishing Star Palace, but now they want you to design one for them.

To enter all you have to do is follow these steps:

Go to **www.secretprincessesbooks.co.uk**

♥ Click the competition module
♥ Download and print the activity sheet
♥ Design a beautiful dress for Charlotte or Mia
♥ Send your entry to:

Secret Princesses: The Sapphire Collection Competition
Hachette Children's Group
Carmelite House
50 Victoria Embankment
London
EC4Y 0DZ

Closing date: 2nd December 2017

For full terms and conditions,
www.hachettechildrens.co.uk/
TermsandConditions/secretprincessesdresscompetition.page

Good luck!

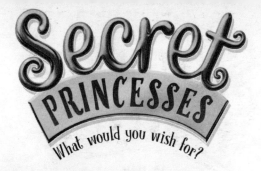

Secret PRINCESSES

What would you wish for?

Lots of fun activities

Create a secret profile

Monthly treasure hunt

Earn princess points

Join in the fun at secretprincessesbooks.com

Secret
PRINCESSES

What would you wish for?

Are you a Secret Princess?

Join the Secret Princesses Club at:

secretprincessesbooks.co.uk

Explore the magic of the
Secret Princesses and discover:

♥ Special competitions! ♥
♥ Exclusive content! ♥
♥ All the latest princess news! ♥

Open to UK and Republic of Ireland residents only
Please ask your parent/guardian for their permission to join

For full terms and conditions go to
secretprincessesbooks.co.uk/terms

Sapphire11

Enter the special code above on the website to receive

50 Princess Points